The Talent Show

This Green Light Reader belongs to:

_____

I read it by myself on:

_____

The Talent Show

A Mr. and Mrs. Green Adventure

KEITH BAKER

sandpiper

HOUGHTON MIFFLIN HARCOURT
Boston   New York

First Green Light Readers edition 2012

All rights reserved. Published in the United States by Sandpiper,
an imprint of Houghton Mifflin Harcourt Publishing Company.
Originally published as a selection in *Lucky Days with Mr. and Mrs. Green*
by Harcourt Children's Books, an imprint of
Houghton Mifflin Harcourt Publishing Company, 2005.

SANDPIPER and the SANDPIPER logo are trademarks of
Houghton Mifflin Harcourt Publishing Company.

Green Light Readers and its logo are trademarks of
Houghton Mifflin Harcourt Publishing Company, registered
in the United States of America and/or other jurisdictions.

For information about permission to reproduce selections from this book,
write to Permissions, Houghton Mifflin Harcourt Publishing Company,
215 Park Avenue South, New York, New York 10003.

www.hmhbooks.com

The text of this book was set in Giovanni Book.
The illustrations were done in acrylic paint on illustration board.

The Library of Congress has cataloged *Lucky Days with Mr. and Mrs. Green* as follows:
Baker, Keith, 1953–.
Lucky days with Mr. and Mrs. Green/Keith Baker.
p. cm.
"Book Three."
Summary: Mr. and Mrs. Green, a loving alligator couple, try their hand at detective work,
a gumball-guessing contest, and the town talent show.
ISBN: 978-0-15-216500-0 hardcover
ISBN: 978-0-15-205604-9 paperback
[1. Lost and found possessions—Fiction. 2. Contests—Fiction. 3. Talent shows—Fiction.
4. Alligators—Fiction. 5. Humorous stories.] I. Title.
PZ7.B17427Mr 2005
[Fic]—dc22 2004005740

ISBN: 978-0-547-85054-2 paperback
ISBN: 978-0-547-86467-9 paper over board

Manufactured in China
SCP 10 9 8 7 6 5 4 3 2 1

4500367835

For Betsy and Chris,

Minna and Cooper,

and their sunshine

Mr. Green turned up the water.
He sang louder—and louder—and *louder!*
No one could hear him sing
in the shower.

Except for Mrs. Green.
She loved listening to him.

He sang all sorts of songs.

(Mrs. Green especially enjoyed opera.)

Every year, Mr. Green performed in the Talent Show.
He had played . . .

the harmonica,   the tuba,

the bongos,   and the triangle.

But this year he would sing.

He had been practicing in the shower every day.

He was ready—

the Talent Show was that afternoon.

Mr. and Mrs. Green hurried to the show.

They watched and waited.

They enjoyed all the performers, especially . . .

the baton twirler
(three batons
at once!),

the ballet dancers
(graceful as swans!),

and the storyteller
(a little Shakespeare,
a lot of Dr. Seuss!).

But their favorite performers of all were the
magician and his assistant.

Mr. and Mrs. Green wanted to try this trick at home.
(It would take a lot of practice.)

Finally, it was Mr. Green's turn.

He walked onto the stage.

He was not nervous—just excited.

So was Mrs. Green.
*What song
would he sing?*

Mr. Green stood still and tall.

He waited for silence.

He waited for inspiration.

He waited to feel the music inside.

Then he took a deep breath and began.

But when he opened his mouth,

nothing came out—

not a note or a noise,

not a peep or a pip,

not a squeak or a squawk.

Mr. Green was soundless.

Soundless . . . songless . . . speechless.

Mr. Green took another deep breath.
He began once more. Again, nothing.

Something was wrong, very wrong.

Oh dear, thought Mrs. Green.
She got an idea.

She ran behind the stage.

She turned on the hose.

She sprayed water over the curtain.

On the other side, the water fell on Mr. Green.
Soon he was completely soaked.

He felt wet.

He felt comfortable.

He felt at home.

He felt like . . .

SINGING!

Mr. Green sang loudly
(with enthusiasm and energy),

he sang softly
(with feeling and emotion),

and then he made up a song
(with a snappy beat—
he was *in the groove*).

When Mr. Green finished, he took a bow.
The audience clapped wildly—
even those who got wet.

They shouted, "*Bravo!*"
(*Bravo* means "hooray" in Italian.)
Mr. Green bowed again.
Then he hurried off to find Mrs. Green.

"Thank you!" said Mr. Green.
"That water did the trick!"
"You're welcome," said Mrs. Green.
"You always sing best
   when you're soaking wet."

"I'll need your help again
   next year," he said.
"Singing?" she asked.
"No," said Mr. Green.
"Dancing . . . the tango . . .

on roller skates!"

About the Author

Keith Baker has written and illustrated many well-loved picture books and early chapter books, including several about the charming and lovable Mr. and Mrs. Green. He lives in Seattle, Washington. Visit his website at www.KeithBakerBooks.com.

Picture Books by Keith Baker

Big Fat Hen

Potato Joe

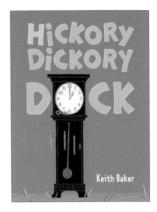

Hickory Dickory Dock

Hide and Snake

Who Is the Beast?

The Magic Fan

Quack and Count

Camping: A Mr. and Mrs. Green Adventure
Keith Baker

Cookies: A Mr. and Mrs. Green Adventure
Keith Baker

Fishing: A Mr. and Mrs. Green Adventure
Keith Baker

The Talent Show: A Mr. and Mrs.
Green Adventure
Keith Baker

George and Martha
James Marshall

George and Martha: Two Great Friends
James Marshall

George and Martha: Round and Round
James Marshall

George and Martha: Rise and Shine
James Marshall

George and Martha: One More Time
James Marshall

Martha Speaks: Haunted House
Susan Meddaugh

Martha Speaks: Play Ball
Susan Meddaugh

Martha Speaks: Toy Trouble
Susan Meddaugh

My Robot
Eve Bunting/Dagmar Fehlau

Soccer Song
Patricia Reilly Giff/Blanche Sims

Catch Me If You Can!/
¡A que no me alcanzas!
Bernard Most

A Butterfly Grows
Steven R. Swinburne

Daniel's Mystery Egg/
El misterioso huevo de Daniel
Alma Flor Ada/G. Brian Karas

Moving Day
Anthony G. Brandon/Wong Herbert Yee

Digger Pig and the Turnip/
Marranita Poco Rabo y el nabo
Caron Lee Cohen/Christopher Denise

The Chick That Wouldn't Hatch/
El pollito que no quería salir del huevo
Claire Daniel/Lisa Campbell Ernst

Get That Pest!/¡Agarren a ése!
Erin Douglas/Wong Herbert Yee

Snow Surprise
Lisa Campbell Ernst

On the Way to the Pond
Angela Shelf Madearis/Lorinda Bryan Cauley

Little Red Hen Gets Help
Kenneth Spengler/Margaret Spengler

Tumbleweed Stew/Sopa de matojos
Susan Stevens Crummel/Janet Stevens
Alma Flor Ada/F. Isabel Campoy